When I'm as

Big as Freddie

by Jocelyn Stevenson
Illustrated by Beverly Phillips

Featuring Jim Henson's
Sesame Street Muppets

A SESAME STREET/GOLDEN PRESS BOOK
Published by Western Publishing Company, Inc.
in conjunction with Children's Television Workshop.

Freddie is my big brother. Someday I'll be as big as Freddie. Then I will be able to do all the things he can do.

When I'm as big as Freddie, I will ride
a two-wheeler.

When I'm as big as Freddie, I will call my best friend on the telephone. I will have very important conversations, just like Freddie.

When I'm bigger,
I will wash my own hair.
I won't get any soap
in my eyes.

Then I will comb out all the tangles
without even saying, "Ouch!"

My big brother Freddie can cross the street without a grownup.

When I'm as big as Freddie, I will look both ways to make sure no cars are coming. Then I will walk across the street without holding anybody's hand.

Freddie can take the bus all by himself.
When I'm as big as Freddie, I'm going to take
the bus, too.

Freddie works hard at school.
When I'm as big as Freddie, I'll bring books home
from school and do homework every day, just like Freddie.

Sometimes Freddie makes my lunch.
When I'm bigger, I will make my own lunch.
I might even make some for Freddie.

Someday I will get my very own library card.
I'll sign my name on the bottom. Then I will
check out two books…or maybe even three!

And someday I will be allowed to stay up as late as Freddie to read all my books.

When I'm as big as Freddie, I'll go to the movies with my best friend.

I'll buy popcorn and we'll share it.

And someday I'm going to camp out in the back yard all night. I won't be scared.

Freddie has his very own bank account.
When I'm as big as Freddie, I will go to the bank,
too. I will say, "May I have a savings account, please?"

When I'm bigger, and have saved some money in the bank, I will buy a present for my mother. I'll pick out a nice present without any help. Then I'll pay for it, just like Freddie.

When I am bigger, I will have a pet mouse, just like Freddie's. I will call him Squeak. I will feed Squeak every day and keep his water dish full. I'll take good care of him.

When I'm as big as Freddie, I will tell our little sister all about being big. Someday she'll be bigger, too.

It won't be long before I'm as big as Freddie.

ABCDEFGHIJK